For Anna,
Catherine, and Blythe,
who inspired me to persist, and
for Eli and Georgia, my everyday inspiration.
—LW

For my parents, Hank and Carol, and
husband Ross, with love and appreciation.
You've helped make my dreams
a reality.
—SC

Copyright © 2010, 2020 by March 4th, Inc.
Text by Land Wilson
Illustrations by Sue Cornelison
Cover and internal design © 2020 by Sourcebooks

Sourcebooks, Little Pickle Press, and the colophon are registered trademarks of Sourcebooks.

Published by Little Pickle Press, an imprint of Sourcebooks Jabberwocky
P.O. Box 4410, Naperville, Illinois 60567-4410
(630) 961-3900
sourcebookskids.com

Originally published as *Sofia's Dream* in 2010 by Little Pickle Press.

Library of Congress Cataloging-in-Publication Data is on file with the publisher.

Source of Production: Leo Paper, Heshan City, Guangdong Province, China
Date of Production: October 2019
Run Number: 5016403

Printed and bound in China.
LEO 10 9 8 7 6 5 4 3 2 1

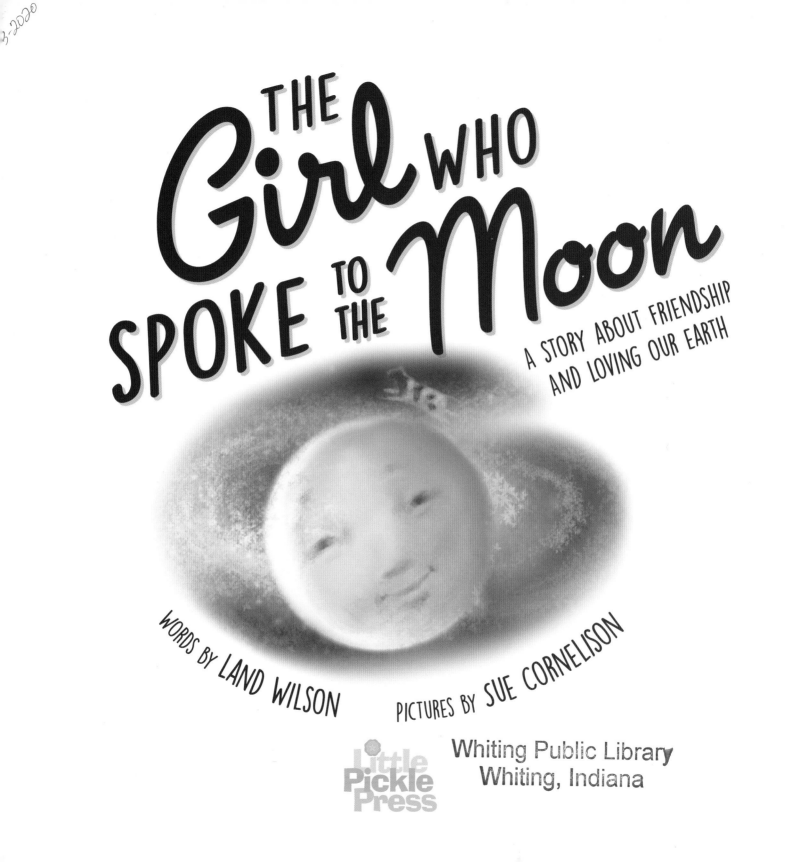

THE Girl WHO SPOKE TO THE Moon

A STORY ABOUT FRIENDSHIP AND LOVING OUR EARTH

WORDS BY LAND WILSON

PICTURES BY SUE CORNELISON

Little Pickle Press

Sofia was a thoughtful girl,
who called the Moon her giant pearl.
As nights passed and the Moon would grow,
she marveled at its opal glow.

One bright night in a dreamy state,
Sofia heard a sound quite late.
She peeked around at all her toys,
and wondered which one made the noise.

When a beam drew her gaze up high,
she saw a face that winked its eye.

"Hello down there," the Moon sang out.
"I hoped to find you peeping out."
"Hello, Moon," she said with a smile.
Then they laughed and talked for awhile.

From this night on, a friendship grew
into a bond both strong and true.

When her friend was only half in view,
    Sofia asked, "Where's the rest of you?"
If he was just a crescent moon,
    she knew that he might vanish soon.

Then one time when the Moon seemed blue,
she noticed that his face was too.
"Excuse me, Moon, what bothers you?
There must be something I can do."

"You need to come and visit me,
for there are some things you must see.
Late tonight, when you're asleep,
dream you'll take a giant leap."

She fell asleep and in her mind,
Sofia left the Earth behind.

And when she reached the Moon in space,
she saw a tear run down his face.
"Now, my friend, that you are here,
I'll show you what it is I fear.
Take a look at Earth with me—
here are the things that you must see."

"Your Mother Earth is where you live.
She is my closest relative.
Also home for nature's wonder,
now she's saddened by real plunder.

"With dirty waters, land, and air,
it looks as though she's in despair.
Her people seem so unaware
that what Earth needs is better care."

"I see now why you feel so sad.
    Polluting Earth is very bad.
I'm glad I came to see your view.
    Please tell me, Moon, what should we do?"

You all should think of Earth each day,
and care for her in every way.
All the little things you do
add up and keep Earth well for you.

"Then work together and you'll see
how wonderful a team can be.
When groups of people work as one,
the most amazing things get done."

"Thank you, Moon,
    for the thoughts you share.
It makes good sense. We need to care!
    I'll tell the world about this dream
        so we can be a better team."

When Sofia woke up from her dream
　　her cares were different, so it seemed.
She made a pledge of things to do
　　like passing on these words to you:

"Earth is the only home we know
　　where living things can breathe and grow.
Let's work together with a plan
　　and save our world, while we still can.

"By far the gift of greatest worth
is our dear home, this planet Earth."

"With dirty waters, land, and air,
it looks as though she's in despair.
Her people seem so unaware
that what Earth needs is better care."

When Sofia visits the Moon in her dreams, the Moon shows her the damage humans are causing to our Earth.

There are over 7.7 billion people on Earth, and that number continues to grow each day. We need to use Earth's resources to help us survive, but we have been using resources in ways that create pollution. The good news is that humans are smart, and when we care about something and work together, we can accomplish big goals—like creating a clean and healthy world.

AIR POLLUTION

Air pollution is caused by burning fossil fuels like coal, gasoline, natural gas, and oil. When we run things that use these fossil fuels, it releases carbon dioxide (CO_2) and other harmful gasses that pollute the air. Our cars (nearly 1.2 billion of them!), trucks, planes, busses, trains, boats, motorcycles, factories, office buildings, schools, and homes all use fossil fuels every day! Air pollution isn't good for us because it causes respiratory diseases like lung cancer and asthma. It can also cause acid rain (which can kill animals on land and in water), reduce the amount of oxygen available (which all living things need to breathe), and cause global warming (or "climate change").

LAND POLLUTION

Land pollution is caused by things like the buildup of garbage in landfills, improper dumping of trash and toxic waste, chemical and oil spills, and using chemicals to farm. It can also happen when large areas of land, like mountains and forests, are removed and destroyed for mining, building cities, and other human uses. Land pollution isn't good for us because we lose valuable land for agriculture, housing, or nature preserves. Land pollution also means our food and water gets polluted, and that can lead to a lot of illnesses like cancer.

WATER POLLUTION

Water pollution is caused by the dumping of industrial waste and toxins that wash into waterways or seep into the ground. Air and land pollution are major causes of water pollution since all those pollutants eventually make their way into our oceans. Water pollution isn't good for us because we need water to drink and polluted water can lead to a lot of diseases. We're also hurting entire ecosystems of plants and animals that we rely on for food. And if we poison our food chain, we are poisoning ourselves.

To help write this book, Land Wilson interviewed three Apollo astronauts. One astronaut, Captain Walter M. Schirra, Jr., told him, "You realize that humans had better learn to be more careful with this one-and-only place we need to live." Here are other quotes from astronauts about what they learned about Earth from being in space:

"I realized up there that our planet is...fragile. That may not be obvious to a lot of folks."
—Alan Shepard, the second man and the first American in space

"This is what heaven must look like. I think of our planet as a paradise. We are very lucky to be here."
—Mike Massimino, NASA Astronaut

"The world itself looks cleaner and so much more beautiful. Maybe we can make it that way—the way God intended it to be—by giving everybody that new perspective from out in space."
—Roger B. Chaffee, NASA Astronaut

TWO

Finding an Idea

I get my ideas from living my life wide-eyed and awake. I sit on the edge of chairs. I pay attention to wherever I am.

—Drew Lamm

One day my friend Karen and her husband decided to surprise their seven-year-old twins. They woke the boys before dawn and drove them to the beach to watch the sunrise. One twin was sleepy and decided to stay in the car. But the other walked out on a rock jetty with Karen. He was mesmerized by the way the light bloomed and shone as the sun came up. At one point they saw a fiery core of light at the horizon. The boy turned to his mother and exclaimed, "Mommy!" He pointed at the horizon. "I can see my soul dancing!"

This is the kind of story that makes us smile. Younger kids say that sort of thing all the time, right? But as we get older we get more rooted in the "real" world. More and more, it matters to us what other people think. So we stop seeing our souls dancing on the horizon. Or, if we do see it, we don't talk about it out loud. And we hesitate to write it down out of fear that someone might laugh at us. That's too bad, because a lot of terrific ideas never get written about.

What do you see? Smell? Dream? Notice? Anything like that can be the spark of an idea to write about. Ideas can jump into your head at the most mundane moments of the day.

"For a long time I thought my ideas lived in

my medicine cabinet in the bathroom," says poet Kristine George. "It seemed as if each time I took out my toothbrush and toothpaste I'd get an idea."

One day you're taking a bath. Suddenly it strikes you that your knuckles look like an elephant's knees. A single thought like that could be the start of a poem.

My ideas often begin like that. I use my writer's notebook to catch ideas for my writing. (If you haven't done so, you should read the book I wrote entitled *A Writer's Notebook: Unlocking the Writer within You.*) I think of my notebook as a net with holes so tiny that no idea can slip through.

A few months ago I was swimming in the ocean. On the ride home I noticed that the dried seawater made my skin feel tight. Later, I jotted this entry into my writer's notebook:

On the way home from the beach, the drying seawater makes my skin feet tight, like all of a sudden it's one size too small for me.

Eventually this thought turned into the following poem:

Driving Home

Our car is a seashell
in an ocean of darkness.

There's sand in my hair,
nose, ears, bathing suit.

I'm coated with dried salt
and my skin feels tight

like it has become one size
too small.

Most of my ideas come from my life, but at times it has taken another person to help me appreciate an idea. About a year ago I had dinner with Eve Bunting, one of my favorite authors. I told her my plans for the Christmas holiday:

"This Christmas my family is going to visit my sister Kathy," I said. "She is very, very pregnant. Her due date is around December twenty-fifth. I think it will be fun for my kids to be with a pregnant woman around that holiday. It might help them experience Christmas in a whole new way."

Eve Bunting leaned forward.

"That's a good picture-book idea," she said with a twinkling smile. I hadn't realized how true this was until she said it.

The topics to write about are as countless as the stars. I believe that the best ideas live inside of us. It's our job to dig them out. Every writer gets stuck from time to time, so here are a few ideas to get your imagination flowing.

Family tradition. This is especially good if your tradition is an unusual one. I have a friend whose family had a ritual for whenever one of the kids lost a tooth. The mother would deposit the tooth in a "tooth bank." There were seven kids in that family, so after a while the bank got pretty full. Think of what a good horror writer would do with an idea like this!

Collections. I know a boy who likes to collect used bandages. Most of them are stained with dried blood. A strange collection like that might provide the seed for a good story.

Special place. When my wife was a girl she used to go to a wardrobe in the basement where her mother's nursing uniforms were hung. The outfits made it look like there was a person in there, and it gave her the willies!

You may have a particular spot—secret passageway, attic nook, the inside of a hollow tree, your grandmother's kitchen—that could provide the setting for a story of your own.

Your place in the family. Are you the oldest? Youngest? An only child? Adopted? Your slot in the family has a great impact on who you are. Listen to this story written by Tanya White, an eighth grader:

My Big Stranger

Last summer my parents went to Hawaii. When they came home they had an unexpected visitor with them. A girl named Mandy. She was tall and pretty and about two years older than me.

"Meet your big sister," Dad said on the driveway.

For a second I just stood there, speechless. Then I turned around and ran up to my bedroom.

Later on the story came out. Dad had a baby with another woman when he was in the military, stationed in Hawaii. That was a few years before I was born but he never told anyone in our family about it, not even Mom. But finally he felt he had to get it off his chest.

"I thought you'd want to know," he told me, and I did, I mean I do. I'm real curious about Mandy. But right now I feel betrayed. I always had a special place—the oldest kid in our family. The first baby Dad played Patty Cake Patty Cake with. The first baby he sung to sleep. Or so I thought.

Moving. Did you leave behind a close friend when you moved from your old house?

Life changes. When I was little, my parents used to plop my sister, brother, and me into the bath together. This seemed quite natural since we were only one year apart. But one day I realized that I didn't want take a bath with my sister. I was too big for that.

Did your big brother go off to college? Did your sister and her baby have to move home to live with you? Was there one night when you realized you were too big to jump into your parents' bed during a thunderstorm? Any change in your life will give you excellent material to write about.

What frightened you when you were little (or what still frightens you)? As a four-year-old I lay in bed, desperately needing to go to the bathroom, but convinced that the moment I stepped out of bed two bony hands would reach out from beneath my bed and grab me by the ankles!

I hope these ideas jog your memory and help you find a rich topic to write about. Lists like this are fun, but the truth is that the best ideas don't appear on any lists of "story starters." The best topics are highly personal, quirky and—well— even a little bit weird. (Anthony, a fifth grader, wrote about his all-time favorite sport: whiffle-ball.)

"Write about what makes you different," says Sandra Cisneros, author of *House on Mango Street.*

Remember: The challenge isn't simply to write about the idea, but to dig down and write about feelings connected to it. Whatever topic you choose, you need to ask yourself: What *angle* will I take when I write about it? Most writers find that broad, general topics don't work nearly as well as topics with a particular angle or focus. Instead of writing all about the beach, write about how the beach looks at sunset. You could write all about sleepaway camp, but you will probably have better results if you narrow your topic to describing the nasty camp food, for instance, or the story of how one annoying counselor drove everybody crazy.

In the following piece, Jessica, a fourth grader, writes about the relationship between her and her little sister. Notice how she focuses her topic around the questions her little sister asks.

My Sister's Silly Questions

My sister's questions are so-o-o-o-o silly. Once she asked me, "How cold is cold?"

I said to my mother: "I'm going to faint." Sometimes my sister is a pest. But I still love her!

Once she asked my mother: "Why do birds fly?"

So my mother said: "That's how they get exercise." Now we know that's not really true. But what do you say to a child who is four years old?

I like my sister's questions because they give me something to think about. Sometimes it's fun answering my sister's questions, other times it's not. Once she asked me: "How come you were born first?" Another time she asked: "Why is the summer called summer?"

Sometimes I get so-o-o-o-o mad I don't know what to say! What's worse, my sister is getting older and the questions are getting harder!

THREE

Brainstorming

I write for a couple of hours every morning. But it's what I do during the other twenty-two hours that allows me to do that writing.

—Don Murray

I recently visited a class of fourth graders.

"Do you know what brainstorming is?" I asked the class.

One boy raised his hand. "Is that sort of like meditating?" he asked.

"Well, not exactly," I said with a short laugh. But then again, maybe it is. Like meditation, brainstorming invites you into a quiet room where you can think deeply about your subject before you start shaping your text.

Brainstorming is sometimes called *prewriting* or even *rehearsal.* Whatever you call it, it refers to all the thinking, preparing, and mental jump-starting that takes place before you start a particular piece of writing. It's a crucial part of what every writer does.

Important: The ideas in this chapter are intended as suggestions only! Some writers do a great deal of brainstorming before they do their actual writing. Other people prefer to simply start writing and see what happens. The start-writing-and-see-what-happens people discover how to organize their thoughts while they write.

What kind of writer are you? Chances are you won't know until you try a few brainstorming ideas. I suggest you read through this chapter and find some ideas that appeal to you. Try these ideas once, and see if they help your writing. If they do, great, use them again. If not, try something else.

I do two kinds of brainstorming. The first kind is open-ended, where I'm casting a wide net, trying to be alert and aware of ideas I might write about. I usually use my writer's notebook for this kind of brainstorming. A writer's notebook gives you an easy, informal, no-pressure place to gather "seed ideas" you can come back to later.

But like most writers, I do another, more focused kind of prewriting that allows me to play with an idea before I actually begin writing. Let's look at several ways you can prewrite on a particular topic. You can use the first one without even touching a pen or a piece of paper.

Talk. When I lived in New York City I often used to invite a friend to meet me at a Hungarian coffee shop. I'd buy my friend a cup of coffee and Danish. In return, he or she would patiently listen while I talked through whatever I happened to be writing about. (I found this especially helpful when I worked on nonfiction articles.)

Talking allowed me to get comfortable with my subject. And I learned to listen to the words I used to describe my subject. At certain times while I talked, my friend would nod, or smile, or lean forward, or seem confused. This told me I needed to give more information or a clearer explanation.

While talking about your writing can be helpful, I'd also be cautious. There is a danger that if you talk about an idea too much you can talk the mystery out of it.

"I'll brainstorm ideas in my notebook, but I never discuss what I'm working on with anyone," poet Kristine George says. "For some reason, talking seems to sap my energy and enthusiasm for an idea of a project."

Author Drew Lamm agrees. "I definitely don't talk to anyone," she says. "If I talk I lose that initial energy that's crucial."

You might want to try this strategy and see if it works for you. In my experience, a little bit of talking goes a long way.

List ideas. Lists are a great way to generate ideas. Remember in the previous chapter I got the idea about how the drying seawater makes your skin feel tight, like all of a sudden it's "one size too small"? At first I wrote that poem and stopped there. But later I returned to the beach with my family. Watching my kids burying each other in the sand and romping in the surf got me thinking about putting together a collection of beach poems. I started by making a list:

General Ideas on a Collection of Beach Poems
Beach Plums (title?)
Hearing the sea when you hold a shell to your ear
seagulls complaint   sandpipers
Waves—tsunami!
Burying my brother
Baby eating sand
Old guy with a metal detector
Nobody argues at the beach, nobody fights
Sandcastles—trying to hold back the sea

This list of beach poems became the start of my recent poetry book, *Have You Been to the Beach Lately?* I think you'll find that lists are an excellent way to generate thinking about any idea.

Make a web. You may have done this before. Put your main idea in the center of the wheel, and make a "spoke" going to each connected idea. I have just begun writing a creative nonfiction book about a local river. My idea is to let the river itself speak through lots of different kinds of writing. To explore my thinking, I sketched the following web:

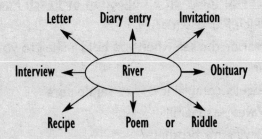

A web like this one is a good way to remind you how much you know about your topic, and to identify gaps where you may need to develop your idea further.

Free write on an idea. The idea of free writing is pretty simple: Don't think, just write! Get a stopwatch or timer. Now give yourself three to five minutes to write. You can write about a topic, or just write whatever comes into your head. Write whatever you want: words, ideas, fragments, phrases.

Separate the words you write with commas or arrows, if you want. The idea is not to let your pen leave the page. Don't think: Write.

You know that nonfiction book I just mentioned about the river? Well, this morning I did a five minute free write on the idea:

> river, river, river, river of water, downriver, tumble down rock stairs, rocks, mossy rocks, slippery, waterfalls, river of moist air on the bridge, white water, white sound, trout, speckled, lamprey river, lamprey eel, eel, leech, bloodsuckers, river animals, river insects, water striders, water bugs, water people, sunbathers at the swimming hole, kayakers, fishermen, man with high rubber boots, walking down river like he's walking down a stream . . .

Three by three by three. My wife JoAnn has had good luck using this idea with her students. She gives them exactly three minutes to write three ideas on each of three topics. This is a great way to jump-start your mind if you're feeling a little groggy. You might look through your writer's notebook for an idea, or pick something you've been itching to write about. You'll want to have a stopwatch handy so you can time yourself.

Try an informal outline. Okay, okay, I know what you're probably thinking: Horrors! Not an outline—anything but that! You noticed that I said an *informal* outline. I'm not talking about the detailed outline with the *I, A, a,* etc. What I'm talking about is a lot simpler and, I think, more useful.

I use an informal outline to help me chunk my ideas before I write. Let's say I'm going to write an information piece about the South American rain forest. A detailed outline probably won't help me, because at the beginning I don't know all the information I'll be gathering. Instead I'll use a simple one. It might look like this:

1) The Rain Forest: Introduction
2) Benefits of Rain Forest
3) Destruction of Rain Forest
4) Conclusion: What Can We Do to Preserve the Rain Forest?

A simple outline like this creates four empty "drawers." Now I'll be able to place each new fact

I gather into the right drawer. This will help me separate ideas and organize my thinking. I know it will be helpful in organizing my writing as well.

If you use an outline, be careful that it doesn't limit your thinking. Writer Ben Mikaelsen says, "I'm not much on outlines because as I write, I get to know my characters better and they end up doing things I could never have predicted with an outline."

Make a time line. This strategy is helpful with narrative writing. I used a time line while putting together the story for my new book *Tommy Trouble and the Magic Marble:*

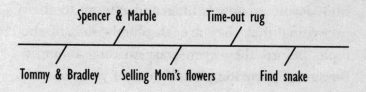

A time line like this can also be helpful when you're working on a biography or writing about historical events. Make a line, and write down when each important event took place.

A brainstorming strategy will help jog your

memory and generate information you might have forgotten. But you need to take it a step further. When you are finished, go back and reread it. Ask yourself these important questions:

Where should I start?
What can I leave out?
How might I organize my material?
For example, which ideas could be clumped together?

Here's the bottom line: Whatever prewriting you do should build your energy to write, not deflate that energy. I've known too many writers who devote so much time and energy to their prewriting that they are absolutely sick of the topic before they even start writing about it! **Beware of prewriting the life out of your topic.** If you feel that happening, stop prewriting and start writing!

Most of the ideas you find in this chapter are done with pen in hand. But I have found that often, my best brainstorming takes place when I'm not writing at all but when I'm just living—

taking a walk, taking a shower, dreaming while I sleep. I might be making a peanut-butter-and-jelly sandwich when all of a sudden an idea jumps into my head. A writer is always alert for ideas that can feed the writing.

FOUR

A Salad of Ideas
by Gordon Korman

When Gordon Korman was in seventh grade, he wrote a novel as an English project. The book, This Can't Be Happening at MacDonald Hall, *got published when he was in junior high! He has written lots of terrific books, including* Liar, Liar, Pants on Fire, The Sixth Grade Nickname Game, *and* Nose Pickers From Outer Space. *Read about how he brainstormed the idea for* The Chicken Doesn't Skate.

I do a lot of school visits, and I turn that into advance brainstorming. Every time I pick up an idea for a story, a character, or even a character name, I type it into a little electronic pocket organizer I travel with. Then, when I'm brainstorming for a novel, I just flip through my "idea file."

A lot of stuff happens in my books, so brainstorming is really important for me. Sometimes, ideas that seem totally unconnected come together in one of my books. My favorite example is *The Chicken Doesn't Skate* (Scholastic). It's about an ice hockey team whose mascot is a chicken. But it really took shape when several "old" ideas from my pocket organizer got kind of mixed up in my head.

First came the chicken story, which I picked up on an author visit in Michigan. It's absolutely, one hundred percent true. A sixth grade science class did a project called "The Complete Life Cycle of a Link in the Food Chain." They adopted a baby chick—just hatched—and raised it in school. They built a mini-chicken coop, signed up for feedings and cleanings, and fought for the privilege of taking their subject home on week-ends. After three months, when the chicken was a fully grown hen, the plan was to kill it, cook it, and eat it. Honest, I'm not making this up. Every student would get one piece of the chicken he or she had helped to raise.

By this time, though, the students had become quite attached to this chicken. They'd watched it grow up, after all. And I suppose a chicken can be cute. They'd even named it—Henrietta. As it sank in that their beloved class pet was really a McNugget-in-training, they caused a huge uproar in their school and, later, the whole town. Even the parents got involved in this major plea for mercy.

That was my original idea, but I knew I needed more. So I flipped through my organizer, and I found this old entry: Switching Narrators. It came from a book I'd read where every chapter had a new narrator. I thought it was so cool that the same events could seem totally different, depending on who was doing the talking. I wanted to try a kids' novel in the same style.

Well, this chicken story was perfect for it. Each narrator could have a completely different view of Henrietta. There could be chicken lovers and chicken haters; a brainy science kid who sees Henrietta as an experiment and nothing more; an animal rights activist; a teacher who is caught in the middle.

Plus—and this is what led to the next idea—if one of the school sports teams became convinced that the chicken was good luck, they would instantly make it their mascot. I chose hockey, and it's not just because I'm Canadian. Hockey players are notoriously superstitious. They would scream twice as loud as anybody else when the time came to take Henrietta to the butcher shop. After all, it can't bode well for a team if somebody fricassees their mascot!

One final "old" idea made the story complete. In my pocket organizer I found an entry called Horror Movie. It was about a kid who writes hilariously bad screenplays for horror films—movies with titles like *Terror In The Sewer*, *Picnic of Death*, and *The Brain-Eaters*. It had nothing to do with chickens or hockey. But it turned out to be the element that tied together all of the other stuff.

I put this writer of horror movies in the class that's doing the chicken project. Suddenly, chickens mysteriously appear in his screenplays. Alien invaders turn out to be interstellar chickens; a mad scientist transmogrifies the entire Super Bowl into poultry. Baffled, he comes to the conclusion that his writing will be haunted forever by chickens if he doesn't protect Henrietta from the frying pan. His participation in the kidnapping gets him recruited by the hockey team as their new goalie. And he wins the championship, saves the chicken, and helps earn first prize in the science fair—all in the same afternoon.

Confused? Trust me, it makes sense when it's down on paper. That's another thing about my brainstorming process. Because so many different ideas get blended together, it's hard to recognize the original seeds in the finished novel. But that's also what makes my job so much fun. The story is alive, always growing, always changing, even writing itself a little bit. I never know for sure how my salad of ideas will get mixed together—at least not until I type the last line on my word processor. But the brainstorming phase is where I try to get the ingredients right.

FIVE

Breaking the Ice:
Getting Started

A journey of a thousand miles must begin with a single step.

—Lao Tsu (sixth century B.C.)

A piece of paper. On some days it seems inviting, like a newly opened box of chocolates. Like the silky surface of your best friend's pool on a hot summer day. But some days it seems to scowl up in an unfriendly way, demanding, *Who do* you *think* you *are, huh? How dare you disturb my perfect empty whiteness?*

You are you. And you have something important to say. But you won't say anything if you don't make a start. You have to begin.

Many writers find that breaking the ice—beginning—is one of the hardest parts of the writing process. As a writer, you face that hurdle every time you sit down to write.

You may be thinking, *Wait. Didn't I already read a chapter called Finding An Idea? Doesn't that break the ice?* Well, yes and no. It's important to have something to write about, but it's also necessary to start writing about it. Those are two separate steps. The world is full of people who will tell you, "I have a great idea for a book [or story]"—but they never quite get around to making a start.

There is a gap between getting the inspiration/idea and beginning to write about it. During that gap, a flock of distractions, doubts, second-guesses, and negative voices come swooping in.

"For me, rough drafting is like facing a monster in the dark," says author Ben Mikaelsen. "As long as the story is still in my head, it is still perfect. When I start writing it becomes flawed, and I struggle."

It's perfectly okay to wait before you start writing about an idea. I have a few ideas that I don't feel quite ready to tackle. But once you know you're ready, it's up to you to make a start. Even a small one.

Write one word. Then another.

On certain days writing the first word feels like sticking my toe into the cold lake. At other times writing even that first word feels like plunging headlong into deep water.

It is important to be gentle with yourself, especially at the beginning. Keep your goals modest. Maybe you're not in good enough shape to do fifty push-ups. But you can do one. And once you do that one, you can probably do a few more. Okay, you did five push-ups today. Tomorrow you can shoot for six, or even seven.

It's exactly the same with writing. You probably won't write too much when you start. One paragraph is fine. Two paragraphs is terrific. A whole page of writing is heroic.

Don't expect profound thoughts or brilliant

poetry to flow out of your pen. If you do, and nothing comes, you'll get so depressed you'll stop writing. Lower your standards enough so you can get something down on paper. And whatever you do, don't beat yourself up if what you write sounds pretty awful. Start. Begin. Write.

Here's the first poem in my book *Ordinary Things:*

Walking
Time to leave my desk
and leave the house,
pulling the door behind.

I write the way I walk
starting out all creaky,
sort of stumbling along,
looking for a rhythm.

Each footstep is like a word
as it meets the blank page
followed by a pause
before the next step:
step, step, word . . .

41

SIX

Going with the Flow

If it is winter in the book, spring surprises me when I look up.

—Bernard Malamud

You start writing something, and you're excited because you think it might turn into a longer story or—who knows?—maybe even a book. Great! But this initial burst of enthusiasm doesn't last very long. Too soon you find yourself getting tired, petering out. The writing is harder than you expected. You get all tangled up in one sentence. The words come slower and slower. Your mind wanders, you get distracted by a TV program, and you abandon the project.

Sound familiar? I'm describing something that happens to all writers. Some writing days get me so frustrated I want to give up writing forever. But it's not as hopeless as it sounds. (See the chapter titled "Writer's Block and Other Monsters" later in this book.) In fact, there are concrete steps you can take to make sure the words keep flowing.

I don't claim to be the greatest writer on Earth. But I have learned that there are definite things you can do to keep the writing flowing so the words add up to something, and you say what you want to say.

Read your way back into an unfinished piece of writing. Yesterday you started a piece of writing. But today when you pick it up again you can't exactly remember what you were thinking, or how you planned to write it. This can be frustrating.

When this happens it can feel like you have to start over, and you can lose interest in the project.

The first thing I do when I return to an unfinished piece of writing? I read what I wrote the day before. I read my words, enjoying the good parts, listening to the rhythms of the words. Often I'll even read it out loud. While doing this, I try to get the flavor of the writing. Now I can continue with what I was working on.

Separate the writing from the correcting. Most people speak about two or three hundred words per minute. But they write much more slowly—maybe twenty words per minute. Let's say while you are writing you stop frequently to look up the spellings of words in the dictionary. That takes a lot of time. Now you're only averaging ten words per minute. Your steady writing flow has been reduced to a mere trickle.

Rough drafting is the time for getting your thoughts down on the paper. Later, you can go back and make sure the spelling, punctuation, and grammar are all correct. But first you need to write words, lots of words.

Let's say I'm working on a rough draft of a

story. I write the word *encyclopedia,* but I'm not sure how to spell it. For now I might just write *enc.,* circle it, and continue writing. Later, I'll return to the word and look it up. I know some young writers who underline a word they know is spelled incorrectly. That way they can easily find the word later when they want to correct it.

The writer Jacqueline Jackson puts it this way. When the fish are biting, you don't stop to clean the fish you have caught. You can do that later. You put another piece of bait on your hook and throw your line back into the water so you can catch more.

It's exactly the same with writing. When your ideas are coming fast and furious, keep your pencil to the paper. Don't do anything to interrupt the flow.

Don't be hyper-critical! Connor writes a sentence, crosses it out, writes another, crosses that out, too. Jill begins by writing three sentences, then crumples up her paper and throws it onto the floor. Melissa erases so often her paper wears through and rips.

Everybody knows writers like this. Try to identify

whatever it is you do that gets in the way of your writing. Many of us have a little voice in our heads that says, *This stinks! This is weak! Hah! A first grader could write better than this!* It's important to silence this voice, gag it, tell it to go away and come back much later.

Relax. Have fun with your writing. Make yourself as comfortable as possible. Being comfortable means feeling like yourself, which is so important if you hope to write anything worthwhile. I know a high-school girl who needs to have a little bowl of apple slices to make herself comfortable while she writes. I find that even having the right clothes matters a great deal. In my closet there are certain flannel shirts, cotton sweaters, and well-worn jeans that I think of as "writing clothes" because I feel so relaxed in them. You may find that it helps to change from school clothes into play clothes before you sit down to write.

Take your time. Many writers get frustrated when their sentences don't come out right. Or they have so many ideas in their heads, they can't possibly get it all on the paper. This can happen to a professional writer, too.

"Sometimes I get overwhelmed by how much more there is to say, especially if I'm writing a short story or novel," says writer Drew Lamm. "I stop myself immediately and say, 'Go back to the last word you wrote. You can write the next word. Then go to the next word after that. . . .' That way I un-overwhelm myself and get back to the work/play at hand."

Count words. Think small. A few sentences makes a paragraph. A few paragraphs makes a page. Even a page or two is a pretty good writing output. Ernest Hemingway, a famous American writer, wrote about two hundred and fifty words—one page daily—but he created a body of work that endures long after his death.

Donald Murray believes that writers need to break big tasks into smaller ones. He is the person who taught me about counting words, a simple technique that has been a huge help to my work, especially when I'm working on a long piece of writing. Yesterday I wrote 798 words of this book. The day before that I wrote 947. Today I have written 374 words, so far. My goal is to write at least 750 words before I quit for the day. I will not finish this book today, but when I write my 750th word I will have the satisfaction of knowing that I reached my goal.

Give yourself a "writing reward." I like to reward myself after I write well or complete a difficult writing task I had been dreading. It doesn't have to be a big thing. I might go to a favorite coffee shop in the afternoon, take a walk, or indulge in a chunk of dark chocolate. Try it. Rewarding yourself is a way of patting yourself on the back and saying, *Good job.* It's important to be your own biggest fan.

Are you still working on a writing project and running out of gas? If so, consider this one final bit of advice:

Make sure your topic interests you. About a year ago, I had what I thought would be a fun idea for a picture book: First Things First. The book would describe all the "firsts" in my life. My first favorite food (besides Mom's milk) was macaroni and cheese. Don't ask me why, but my first word was *bazooka.* And the first thing that frightened me was the vacuum.

I began to write *First Things First,* and had

gotten about halfway through when I began to run out of steam. It had seemed like a cute idea when I first thought of it, but the more I wrote the more I realized how little it interested me. At this point an alarm started ringing in my head, because I have learned that if I'm not interested in what I'm writing about, my readers won't be much interested, either. Quickly, thankfully, mercifully, I pulled the plug and abandoned this story.

Katherine Paterson says there must be an "emotional core" at the heart of every good poem or story. In other words, the writer needs to write it from deep inside. If that emotional core is missing, and the writing is going badly, it may be a signal that it's time to seek a different topic to write about.

Think of writing as talking on paper. Imagine that you are seeing your favorite cousin for the first time in four months and you can't stop talking. Try to get that same talky feeling when you put your pencil to the paper. Let the words flow. I give lots of suggestions for writing with voice in my book *Live Writing: Breathing Life into Your Words*.

If you're lucky, you will get to a point while writing where you lose track of time, you stop worrying about the spelling, and you lose yourself in the material. At that moment, the line between "work" and "play" vanishes, the outside world disappears, and you're aware of nothing but the world you are creating with words. That's a terrific feeling, and the more you write the more you will feel it. I call it living inside a story (or poem), and it's a wonderful place to live.

SEVEN

Interview with Drew Lamm

Drew Lamm's books include The Prog Frince: A
Mixed-Up Tale, Sea Lion Roars, *and the short story*
"Stay True" *in the anthology* Stay True: Short Stories
for Strong Girls *compiled by Marilyn Singer. Her writing
style is a mirror of Drew herself: funny, warm, playful,
witty, energetic, and full of wonderful wordplay.*

Why do you write? I mean, what's in it for you?

Writing is the possibility of falling in love. Every time I pick up my pen there's the chance that I'll have that astonishing feeling. Because I never know when a poem or story will emerge with a perfect fit. And I'll be delighted by it. Love it. Want to read it over and over again. And feel amazed that it's here somehow because of me.

When I write, parts of my soul emerge. It's like peering at a water droplet under a microscope—life appears that you couldn't see before. There's hidden life inside of us and writing is the microscope that reveals it.

Where do you tend to get your ideas?

I get my ideas from living my life wide-eyed and awake. I sit on the edge of my chair. I pay attention to wherever I am. My writing notebook is with me most always, and I often think

I'm a much more interesting person with my notebook than without because it keeps me alert. With paper at hand, any idea that flies by gets a place to land.

Sometimes a line of prose or poetry will bump into me almost as a physical sensation and I know that if I write it down immediately and follow after it, something will be there. Other times I hear a phrase spoken or read a line of poetry that moves my mind into a new place, and suddenly I want to follow these new ideas.

What kind of prewriting/brainstorming do you find helpful? Do you outline? List? Make a web?

No! I know there are writers who organize all over the place. I'm not one. And I definitely don't talk to anyone. Ideas bring with them an energy to write them. If I talk about them instead, I lose that initial energy that's crucial.

Most all my beginnings or rough drafts start in my notebook. Once I begin to see the shape of what I'm writing, I often switch over to my computer. Except with poetry. I stay with pen and ink 'til the very end with poetry.

Lots of writers find it hard to start writing. Do you?

Usually I start because I have a strong feeling deep in my gut that I have to begin something. An idea hits me—whonk—and I have to follow it and write.

When it's a normal-nothing-knocking-on-my-brains kind of day I read poetry to get me off the ground and up into flight. Or I write a bunch of slop and don't worry about it. I figure I'm just exercising. On the days I just write a bunch of slogging muck, I don't let it bug me. There'll be other days.

Do you stick to a regular schedule?

I hate regular schedules—too predictable!

Boring. But I do tend to be more productive from eight A.M. to two-ish and then again later on at night, when the house gets quiet and I can remember who I am and sink into the silence.

How do you keep the writing going?

I read. I celebrate the thought that I'm a writer and that ideas are infinite and friendly.

While reading a long story I vanish from the chair I'm sitting on, the room I'm in, the time of day. A computer helps me vanish some-how—my fingers don't get cramped so soon and I'm not as aware of my hands.

What kinds of revisions do you typically do?

I'm wild for revising. Love it. It's like playing! The best part. The scary part is getting out that first draft, because you don't know if you have a creature worth playing with. Once you discover that you have something, you can stop sweating and start messing around with it—revise.

I love finding the ordinary bits of prose and surprise them, shine them up, rattle their bones until something emerges that's worth sinking your reading teeth into. I try to cut out chunks of words that don't make the words quiver.

Could you say anything else about your writing process?

I rarely play music while I write because it reminds me of this world and I want to vanish into my story. Being a writer is a way to be invisible, a wildly alert spy.

I need a lot of white space—still, quiet times, where I can disappear into myself and hear the beat of my own heart.

EIGHT

Rereading

When you read, you get the great pleasure of discovering what happened. When you reread, you get the great pleasure of knowing where the author's going and seeing how he goes about getting there.

—Shelby Foote

The letter Q must always be connected to the letter U in order to make a word. In the same way, this chapter on rereading should be bundled together with the one on revision, which follows. I originally planned to combine them into one big mega-chapter, and decided it would be too long. But I hope you will think of them as two halves of a whole.

You may be thinking, *Wait a sec. What's the deal? This is a book on* writing, *not reading!* But learning how to reread your words is a crucial part of the writing process. The Shelby Foote quote (above) refers to reading, but I believe it relates just as much to writing. You need to spend time rereading your drafts, deciding what works well, what could be better. That's a necessary step before you can make changes in your text.

I'll tell you a secret: Most young writers don't reread what they have written. They skip over that all-important step. Too many times I've seen a student write a page or two and immediately raise his hand, motioning me over, asking, "Will you read this?" Or, "Is this good?"

You need to be the world's greatest expert on

your own writing. And the way you do that is by rereading the words you have written down. If you learn nothing else about writing this year, learn how to reread your words.

You need to wear two hats: a writing hat and a rereading hat. (I know, hats aren't allowed in your school, but anyway . . .) Skilled writers alternate the hats they wear—first writing, then rereading, often switching back and forth many times while writing a single piece. Lucy Calkins, a writer and teacher, calls this "passion hot, critic cold." In your role as writer you should be passionate, but in your role as reader you need to stand back and coolly decide where the writing works well and where it could be strengthened.

Yesterday my son Joseph, who is six, had a new friend come to our house. I was curious about how the visit would go. In the past my son has had a tendency to be so focused on what *he* wanted to do that he didn't pay enough attention to his friend. But this time the two first graders had a blast playing together all afternoon. As the boy was leaving to go home, Joseph called to him, "I hope you had fun!" His friend smiled and nodded.

This story reveals an important truth about writing. Many people write the way little kids play with their friends—totally focused on themselves. It's an important step when a writer becomes aware of the reader. "I hope you had fun!" is important for playing with your friend, but it's just as important when you write. You want to have fun when you write, but you want your reader to have fun, too.

You read a paragraph. Later, when you have to answer three questions based on the paragraph, you go back and reread the passage. We all know about that kind of rereading. But I'm talking about a different kind of rereading. When you reread your own unfinished writing, you start thinking about the person who will read your words. This may lead you to ask certain questions:

- What parts will the reader enjoy? Where does the writing sound good and work well?
- Are there any places where my reader might get confused? Do I wander off my topic?
- Have I left out information the reader needs in order to understand what I'm trying to say?

It takes a long time to get good at rereading your writing. At first it may feel awkward trying to read your own words from the perspective of another reader. Here are a few tips for making this work:

Build on strengths. When I reread my work I first try to identify the good parts. Often it's not much, only a sentence or two. I challenge myself to make the rest of the piece worthy of those places where the writing really sings.

Reread with pencil in hand. That way you can mark places for possible changes. Victoria, a seventh grade writer, uses those yellow Post-its as she rereads. She jots notes to herself, sticks them to her draft, and uses them as a guide during the revision process.

I like this idea, though I don't tend to use Post-its. As I reread, I write codes in the margins to help me get ready to revise. I make a large ! in the margins where it sounds good; I'll put a big ? where I'm afraid it might sound confusing. I might even write myself a note—**"Say this better"**—where the words sound rough or awkward. I've noticed that rereading with a pencil in hand makes me more alert.

Don't fixate on spelling mistakes. You can always go back later and fix the spelling, grammar, etc. In this chapter I'm talking about an open-ended, imaginative kind of rereading in which you stand apart from your words and try to figure out ways to make them even better.

Reread it out loud. If you're in class, you will want to do this with a soft voice so you don't disturb people around you. As you reread, don't just look at what the words mean, but also *listen to the sound of the words.* Reading out loud helps you to get the sound of your words in your head.

I have been working on a playful story for young readers that will be titled, "Where can you find a new nose?" The first page goes like this:

Imagine one day you need
New body parts.
Where might you look?
Where would you start?

If you need a spare leg
Try the leg of a table.

If you need a new eye
Try the eye of a needle.
If you need a new neck
Try the neck of a bottle.
But where can you find a new nose, a new nose?
Who knows where to find a new nose?
You'll find a new tongue
In the tongue of a shoe

. . . etc.

After finishing a draft of this story I reread what I'd written and asked myself, *Where does the writing sound good and work well?* Mostly, I liked it. The idea sounded fresh, clever. I thought kids would enjoy the wordplay and double meanings, and I could visualize illustrations to go with the words.

I read it again and this time asked myself, *Where does the writing need work? Where does it sound different from how I want it to sound?* A phrase at the beginning caught my eye. *New body parts* seemed somehow wrong. The book I was trying to write was supposed to be light, funny, playful. *New body parts* sounded ghoulish and a bit sinister. That would be fine for a horror story, but it didn't fit with the flavor of the book I envisioned.

Rereading the manuscript prompted me to change the beginning. Notice the difference between the two versions.

ORIGINAL BEGINNING	REVISED BEGINNING
Imagine one day you need	If you need some replacements
New body parts.	If you need something new
Where might you look?	Here's how you can find
Where would you start?	Extra pieces of you.

Steven, a fifth grader, wrote a story draft that went like this:

I love to go to my Uncle Mack's house because there's nobody bossing me around. I can cook popcorn or make a snack whenever I want. I don't have to do any chores. I get to stay up as late as I want. I sleep until noon in the morning, and the first thing I do when I wake up is blast the stereo in my bedroom.

Steven didn't see anything wrong with this beginning when he looked at his paper. But when he read it out loud he heard that each sentence began with *I.* He realized that the repetition would be annoying to a reader. This prompted him to go back and vary the way his sentences began:

I love to go to my Uncle Mack's house because there's nobody bossing me around. Uncle Mack lets me cook popcorn or make snacks for myself whenever I want. Nobody makes me do any chores. I get to stay up as late as I want. Most mornings I sleep until noon, and the first thing I do when I wake up is blast my stereo.

I realize that many students enjoy writing on a computer. Computers can make writing more fun, but there are certain dangers, too, especially when it comes to rereading. Many kids find that rereading a story on a computer can be a real challenge.

Jeff, a fifth grader, told me, "When I write on the computer it's like TV writing. I mean, on the screen the sentences always look right, even when they need a lot of work." If you are working on a computer, you may need to get up, stretch, wash your face, even get a breath of fresh air before you go back to it. It also helps to print what you have written so you have a paper copy to reread.

Rereading your writing is like making an author study of yourself. You learn how you tend to begin a story, which words you love to use, etc. You discover what you do well, and what you need to work on. In a way, you become your own personal coach. That's a great thing to have, but don't be too hard on yourself. Never forget that the most important skill a coach can have is patience.

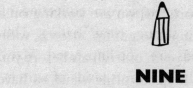

NINE

Revision: Radical Surgery

*I love revising but I don't think of it as rewriting.
I see it as layering. I keep adding layers to my
book, each time concentrating on a different area
such as characters, detail, plot, description, etc.*
                                        —Ben Mikaelsen

Revision. *Re-vision.* The word means "to see again."
It's important to step back from your writing once

in a while and take a new look at it. That "new look" often happens when you reread your words, as we saw in the previous chapter. Revision hinges on that rereading.

When it comes to revision, teachers and students have a difference of opinion. Teachers insist that revision is the best part of the writing process—a chance to reshape your collection of ragtag sentences into strong, clear writing. This sounds good, but kids are not impressed. Many students are one-draft, only-draft kinds of writers, I-said-it-how-I-want-it-the-first-time-and-I-definitely-don't-want-to-copy-it-over-again kinds of writers. Many young writers dislike revision, and consider it about as much fun as washing a sinkful of dirty dishes. By hand.

"Revision is boring," Anthony told me. "I mean, you gotta go back and recopy all those words . . ." He sighed and rolled his eyes.

But for me revision is more than dull recopying. Revision lies at the heart of my process. "I'm not a very good writer," somebody once said, "but I'm a pretty good reviser." That sounds like me. I think of revision as "story surgery," a time when I roll up my sleeves and make the dramatic changes necessary to make my words sing to the tune I want.

In this chapter I want to explore revision: what it is, how to make this powerful tool work for you, and how to make it fun. I'm going to share some of the ways I revise my writing. No, you won't use all of these, but maybe you'll get a revision idea you hadn't considered before.

Some writers find that they need to write a first draft before they can reread it and can figure out how they want to reshape it. Other writers make revisions while they write. Remember: There's no one way to do it.

Layering. Often you reread your writing and realize that you have left out important information or a description that would give the reader a clearer picture of what's going on. You can go back and add it the second time around.

Wayne Wilson, a fifth grader, was working on a story about his little sister. Here is the beginning:

My Baby Sister

I've got a baby sister named Heather. She's five months old. She smiles a lot, especially when my brother and I play peekaboo with her. She can almost sit up, and she likes it when we read books to her. But sometimes she tries to chew on the pages.

In a writing conference, Wayne and I talked about what he'd written.

"What does your sister look like?" I asked him.

"I don't know," he said, shrugging. "Like a baby, I guess."

"My friend's baby was born with thick black hair," I told him. "Does your sister have lots of hair like that?"

"No, none!" Wayne said with a laugh. "Her head is real smooth, like a little bowling ball!" I suggested he might want to go back and describe for the reader what the baby looked like. Look at how adding this description changes the story:

The Little Baldie

My sister is five months old. Her name is Heather. She's cute even though she doesn't have any hair. Her head is smooth as a bowling ball. My uncle bought a little pink hair bow for her, but there was no hair to clip it on! My mother took some scotch tape and taped it to the top of her head! Dad likes to call her the little baldie. Whenever he says that, Heather gives him a big smile.

Not only did Wayne add description to his story, he changed the title, too. I think the new title, "The Little Baldie," is a lot more intriguing than the first one he had.

When you are layering like this, your writing will probably get longer. But that's not the point. The real trick is to go deeper into what you are writing about. Try it. While writing a second draft try to remember other details, incidents, or thoughts that will make your writing richer and more detailed.

Change from one kind of writing to another. At times I'll reread a story and realize I'm trying to force the writing into the wrong genre. (This word, *genre*, means form or kind of writing.) For instance, I realize that my story might work better as a poem, or maybe as an essay.

Change the beginning. Casey Gordon is a fourth grader in Dublin, Ohio. He was working on a piece about John Elway's last game before he retired. It began, "For the last time, John Elway came onto the field."

This didn't sound right, so Casey made several changes. He wanted the readers to understand how sad it was both for Elway to leave and for Casey to watch him on the field. Instead of moving on and coming back to it later, Casey reworked the lead until it sounded like this:

"John Elway came onto the field and said his good-byes to his team and the game and the fans he loved. When they retired his number, his wife fell in tears. The last half time he would be on the field."

Casey likes this lead better, but he is still in the process of revising the phrase "when they retired his number," because it doesn't say what he wants it to. He thinks it would be more powerful to know that "No one will ever wear Number Seven again." Now he is trying to work that line into his lead.

Prune your writing. A few years ago we had a yard with a fabulous patch of raspberries. It produced so many berries, we had to give them away to friends. (We seemed to have extra friends around at that time of the year!) One year I hired a man to prune our raspberries. He came one autumn morning, and when he finished I was astonished by how much he had cut. There was almost nothing left!

"Don't you think you cut too much?" I stammered.

"No," he said, smiling. "Raspberry bushes are like rosebushes. When you prune 'em, they come back stronger than ever the next year." He was right: The next year our raspberry harvest was bigger than ever.

You need to prune your writing, too. As you reread your writing, look at your words with a cold eye. What passages are extra, repetitive, or unnecessary? Where do you wander off the topic? Often there is a particular passage that you needed to write, but does the reader need to read it? Cut it. The reader would silently thank you.

Revise your voice. In this book I'm trying to make the voice sound relaxed and informal, like you (the reader) and I are having a conversation. But sometimes when I reread what I've written it doesn't sound like me at all. For example, in a first draft of this chapter, I wrote:

Skilled writers frequently reread their writing and try to envision what they were originally trying to say.

Yuck! That sentence sounded awfully stiff, formal, and wordy. I decided to revise the sentence to make it sound more conversational:

It's important to step back from your writing once in a while and take a new look at it.

At times you will want to change your writing to make it funnier, livelier, more sarcastic, etc. There will be other times when you'll want to revise your writing in the opposite direction. If you are writing a complaint letter, for example, you may want to use a more formal voice.

Change the point of view. Have you ever had trouble writing about something that felt too personal? I have. If you don't have much luck writing about it from the first person *I*, try rewriting it from the *he* or *she*, as if it happened to someone else. This is called the third person point of view, and it can give you distance from subjects that are painful or emotional.

Change the tense. Most writers work in the past tense, "Last summer I went to see my grandmother . . ." But switching to the present tense can give your writing a startling sense of immediacy. In a story I'm working on, I wrote this passage:

When I walked into the kitchen I saw Uncle Joey sitting at the table. His tie was loose around his neck, and there was a look on his face I'd never seen before.

"What's wrong?" I asked.

He stared up at me through a curtain of cigarette smoke . . .

Look what happens when I write the same passage using the present tense:

When I walk into the kitchen I see Uncle Joey sitting at the table. His tie is loose around his neck, and there is a look on his face I've never seen before.

"What's wrong?" I ask.

He stares up at me through a curtain of cigarette smoke . . .

I do many other kinds of revisions in addition to those I've listed here. I change the ending or change the order of what I've written (maybe starting in the middle or at the end of the event I'm describing). Often I realize that my topic is too large, and I need to break it into smaller chunks or chapters. One of my favorite strategies is to slow down the "hot spot," or crucial moment of the story, using dialogue, emotion, and frame-by-frame detail. Writer Barry Lane calls this "exploding a moment," and it's a terrific way to create a scene at a crucial moment in the writing. I explore many of these ideas in my book *Live Writing: Breathing Life into Your Words.*

Whatever changes I make in my writing, I find that they take time, and time seems to be scarcer and scarcer these days. During school hours, students are too often expected to make "instant revisions." These on-the-spot revisions usually turn into first aid, putting a Band-Aid on the writing instead of doing the deep surgery that is necessary. When you truly revise your writing you have to revise your thinking, and that may take a lot longer than five or ten minutes.

Often I'll send a manuscript to my editor and she'll respond by saying, "This is going to be good, but I think you should put it away for a while. Come back to it in a month or two." Later, when that time has passed, I find that I have the fresh eyes that help me to look at my writing with a new perspective.

Many students think of revision as a way to fix a broken piece. That can be true. But I think of it as a way to honor a strong piece of writing. Let's say I have three rough drafts in front of me. The rough draft of story A is just average. The rough draft of story B is terrible. But I know the draft for story C has a real spark. What to do? Chances are good that I will revise story C, the one that has potential.

You don't have to revise everything you write. If you write something that doesn't interest you, try to finish it, but feel free to go on to what you really want to write about. Find a subject you can really sink your teeth into.

"I only revise pieces that are worth spending time with," writer Drew Lamm says, "so if I'm revising it's because I feel I have something wonderful here."

Revision isn't boring. It is life and death surgery, and it can look messy or downright *bloody*. That creature who is struggling for breath on the operating table is Your Writing, a patient who will live or die depending on what radical amputations, grafts, stitching, or other changes you perform during the operation.

It's up to you, Doctor.

TEN

Interview with Ben Mikaelsen

*Ben Mikaelsen has written some terrific adventure books
for kids. They include Rescue Josh McGuire, Sparrow
Hark, Red, Stranded, Countdown, and Petey.
Here's how Ben writes his books.*

Why do you write? What compels you to do so?

I'd have to say that writing is a compulsion.

Since I was young I have laid awake at night with ideas bonking around inside my head. Writing helps me put ideas to rest.

Where do you get your ideas?

I tend to start with a setting like Africa, or space, and then the story grows out of that place. Over a year or two period, the story comes together in my mind, and I start writing.

Do you work from an outline?

No, I'm not much on outlines, because as I write, I get to know my characters better, and they end up doing things I never could have predicted with an outline.

How do you work? Do you stick to a regular schedule?

When I'm rough drafting I try to drop off the world into a little cabin or something. I like to live with characters and not be disturbed when I'm creating them. The rewriting process is easier. I can sit and edit anywhere, grabbing time on the run.

Do you ever run into writer's block?

With writer's block, I just start writing about anything: dirty socks, itchy noses, etc. When my mind gets going, I'm back in business.

How would you describe your editing process?

I try to polish my manuscript as smooth as I can, like a rock. The finer I polish, the smaller the scratches I can see. A good editor can help me see scratches I didn't notice.

Do you have a particular writing place? What is your space like, and how do you use it?

Every writer I know seems to have a different "way" and place to write. I find that the actual process of writing is not healthy. Think about it—sitting in front of a computer screen fantasizing eight hours a day for three months. They lock people up for that! For this reason, when I finish rough drafting, I try to get out of Dodge! I make sure to get out of the house and go camping, traveling, whatever, just to get my mind out of the hole. I have a waterfall near our house that I love to visit and edit beside it.

Because rough drafting comes the hardest to me, I try to isolate myself as much as I can. I find I am not very social during this period of about three months. After that I can edit in a traffic jam if needed. I've written books while I've traveled four months through South America, and I've written books holed up in a little cabin near Yellowstone Park for two months.

I use a notepad and a small tape recorder to capture thoughts when I'm in the woods or driving. One of my dreams is finally coming true. We are building a small cabin near the house, a "writing center" with one whole wall of glass facing the woods. There is no tele-phone, and the only windows in the cabin face away from the house and the road. I look for-ward to writing my next book in this setting. Somehow I think writing will always be a very difficult matter regardless of where we plop ourselves.

You do a lot of research, right?

Yes, I take about two months each year to research. Maybe half of my research benefits the book directly. The other half is for me. I want to make sure I grow with each book and don't just regurgitate the same thing over and over in different settings.

Any advice for young writers?

I'm often asked how to become a better writer. I always say, Go out and live the most exciting life you can, and never quit writing about it. Don't mix up the order!

ELEVEN

Proofreading

I think editing is the easiest part. You've already sweated out the literature, the story, the loops and curls. You've perfected the music and now you just have to check for the obvious stuff: spelling, grammar, all that. And if it's not obvious to you, this is the one part where someone else is welcome to jump in and help!

—Drew Lamm

Imagine that you are acting in a play. You spend weeks learning your lines, practicing while standing on the stage of an empty theater. During those rehearsals would you wear makeup and costumes? Use props? Probably not. It wouldn't make sense to do all that until the seats were filled with real people watching the play.

The same thing is true in writing. Proofreading becomes important when you move from private to public with what you have written. When the time comes for someone other than yourself to read your sentences, you will want them to be correct.

Proofreading is another kind of rereading. But instead of rereading for meaning, you reread for correctness. Here are some simple steps you can take to proofread your writing, and even have a tad of (dare I say it?) fun while doing so.

To many writers, proofreading feels overwhelming. They get lost in all the sentences, all the mistakes, etc. I'd suggest you start with an editing checklist. A checklist keeps you focused on what you're supposed to be looking for.

Keep your editing checklist short. The longer the checklist, the less useful it will be. For now you might proofread for ending punctuation (? . !), capital letters, paragraphing, spelling. You can always add to this checklist at a later time.

When I work with young writers I suggest they try the following trick. Use a different color marker to proofread for each skill:

1) Ending punctuation (Red)
2) Capital letters (Green)
3) Paragraphing (Orange)
4) Spelling (Blue)

While holding the red marker, proofread your writing, making sure you ended each sentence with the right punctuation. If not, make the corrections using the red marker. I like to use red for this skill because red is the color of stop signs and red lights. In the same way, the ending punctuation tells the reader that he or she has reached the end of the sentence.

When you finish proofreading for ending punctuation put down the red marker. Pick up the green marker and make sure you have capitalized those words that need to be capitalized. Why green? Because my birthday is St. Patrick's Day, and green is my favorite color. But on a more serious note, the color green says "Go," and a capital letter at the beginning of a sentence tells the reader to go ahead. Make sure you've capitalized the first letter in proper names, months, days of the week, etc. If not, make your corrections using the green marker. Each time you proofread you will use a different color, and you will reread the piece of writing looking for that particular type of correction only.

Don't you hate reading books where there are long blocks of text and no paragraph breaks to give your eyes a chance to rest? I do. And now you can do something about it. Pick up the orange marker and make sure you have broken up your writing into the appropriate paragraphs. You need a new paragraph when:

- you introduce a new idea
- time has passed
- a new person begins speaking

Mark the places where you know you need to have a new paragraph. Some writers use the paragraph sign (¶) to do this.

That leaves spelling. Pick up your blue marker. This time I want you to read your piece of writing *backwards*. That may sound crazy, but try it. That's the way professional proofreaders check for spelling. I find that when I check my spelling while reading frontwards, I tend to get caught up in what my story is about. If you proof-read by reading backwards, you've got a much better chance of identifying misspelled words. You can underline or circle any word you didn't spell correctly.

If you write on a word processing program, you may use a computerized spell checker. But beware: While the computer can identify mis-spellings, it probably can't tell when you're using a word incorrectly. For example, if I write *heavan*, my spell checker automatically underlines the word in red to tell me I've spelled it wrong. It asks me if I would like it to automatically correct this word, and of course I say yes, so that the word will be correctly spelled, heaven. But look what happens if I write this sentence: "To day I red the newspaper."

See what I mean? There are mistakes in this sentence, but my spell checker didn't catch them because all of the words used in this sentence actually exist. The problem, in this case, is that the words are used incorrectly. The sentence should read, "Today I read the newspaper."

Think of your eyes as rakes trying to pick out as many writing mistakes as possible. Be nice to yourself. Nobody's perfect. If you find five errors—good. If you find eight errors—even better. You won't find them all, but do the best you can.

Before you make a final copy, give the writing to someone who can give it one last careful proofreading. After all this hard work, you don't want any glaring errors to mar your writing. A parent, relative, or teacher can be your final editor. But it could also be a kid you know in school. In one fourth grade class I visited there was a girl named Victoria who was nicknamed the "Queen of Quotations." Victoria could quickly teach the other students how and when to use quotation marks in their writing—even better than the teacher!

If you're like me, you probably won't edit everything you write. I don't go back to correct the spelling in my writer's notebook, for example. That's personal writing I don't share with anybody. But I want to make my writing as error-free as possible if someone is going to take the time—and make the effort—to read it.

Proofreading your writing allows you to make your writing smooth and reader friendly. If your words are correctly spelled and punctuated, anybody in the world who reads English will be able to enter the world you have created. If you have done your job well, your reader may even forget that he or she is reading a story. The experience of reading your work will feel real. At that point you'll have the satisfaction of knowing that someone is living in a city of words. A city you built yourself!

TWELVE

Publishing: Going Public

Dear Mr. Fletcher,
Howdy! I just finished reading your book
Spider Boy. *I really don't much like to read.*
Mostly I like to stay outside, hunting and fish-
ing, but your book wasn't nearly as boring as I
expected it to be.

—Jake "The Snake" Wilcox,
sixth grade

If you have ever wondered what it's like to be a published author, consider the following story.

Once, on a flight from Boston to Denver, I was walking down the aisle to get a magazine when suddenly I noticed one of the passengers reading one of my books. I was amazed, thrilled! I went over to the woman and introduced myself.

"I wrote that book," I told her, grinning like an idiot.

The woman gave me a skeptical look. She didn't believe me! I didn't know what to do so I reached into my wallet and fished out my driver's license to prove that I was Ralph Fletcher. When she saw my license she nodded and apologized.

"Sorry," she said. "Hey, this is a good book."

"Thanks," I said. Somehow, the fun had gone out of it.

Getting published isn't all that it's cracked up to be. Yes, it's nice to see my books in a bookstore, and to get an occasional letter from a young reader. But too many people think that getting published is the frosting on the cupcake, the sweetest part. They're wrong. Getting published won't make you an instant celebrity. First and foremost, you should be writing because you want to write.

My friend Tom is a fine cook. He reads *Gourmet* magazine. He's got hundreds of spices in his cabinets, including lots of hot sauces and weird stuff you've never heard of. He loves to try out different recipes. His friends eagerly await their turn to be invited to his house for dinner.

Does Tom have his own restaurant? Nope. But that doesn't make him any less of a wonderful cook. He cooks because he loves food.

In the same way, getting published doesn't make you a writer. A writer is a person who loves words, loves to write, and *does* write on a regular basis.

Having said all that, I will admit that it's nice to see your name in print. More than nice. It's TERRIFIC! Above all, writing is a form of communication, and it's wonderful knowing that an actual flesh-and-blood person will read your words!

Publishing a poem, story, or book is such an intoxicating thing that you can lose perspective if you're not careful. I know a young man who made a list of his goals for the year (he's fifteen). At the top of his list he wrote, "Publish a book this year." It's great to aim high, but publishing a book may be an unrealistic goal when you're fifteen years old. It's very, very rare to get a book published when you're that young. True, Gordon Korman published his first novel when he was in junior high, but that's almost unheard of.

Don't rush it.

Now isn't the time to try to make a zillion dollars writing the next blockbuster wizard series, or trying to become the next Stephen King. There's plenty of time for that. You've got your whole life ahead of you.

On the other hand, the time may come when you write something that you feel is pretty good, and you want other people to read it. When it comes to publishing your writing, you've got lots of options. Here are just a few:

• School newspapers, yearbooks, and local newspapers usually publish student work. Read a sample copy, and find out exactly what they're looking for.

• Magazines like *Cricket, Stone Soup,* and *Merlin's Pen* publish student writing. Go to the library and read a few sample copies of the magazine before you send them any writing. (One book I would highly recommend is *Market Guide For Young Writers* by Kathy Henderson, Betterway Publications, Inc., PO Box 219, Crozet, Virginia. This book has lots of great ideas for getting published, and includes the addresses of many magazines that publish student work.)

• Check out contests put on by local bookstores, magazines, organizations, or national groups.

• See if you can get your teacher interested in a classroom or school-wide Author's Day celebration. I participated in such a day at a school in New York City. All the students prepared published versions of their best stories, poems, and nonfiction pieces. They worked hard putting together written invitations to their parents, grandparents, local reporters, even the superintendent of schools. When the big day arrived, each class had its own celebration, where every student got a chance to read aloud to the gathered audience. (The adults wrote responses to each student on index cards.) Teachers paired up classes of different aged students where kindergarten kids read their pieces to fourth graders, for example, and vice versa. The PTA had bought a huge cake that said CONGRATULATIONS AUTHORS. The energy in that building was sky high that day. It was a day nobody would forget for a long time.

Whenever you submit your work for publication, you should present it with all the care you can muster: typed or written in your neatest writing on clean, unsmudged paper. And the writing shouldn't have any spelling or grammar mistakes.

There are lots of different ways of getting published. You don't have to win first prize in a writing contest or get your poem in a glossy magazine. Even if you don't want to open your restaurant to the public, you can still cook up something delicious for people who will appreciate it.

As you work on a particular piece of writing, ask yourself, Who should read this? Who is my target audience for what I'm writing? This question may steer you toward a kind of "going public" you may not have imagined.

Elizabeth, an eighth grader from Texas, was working on a story about her search to find her biological parents. I was impressed with how much information she had been able to weave into her writing.

"You know a lot about this, don't you?" I said.

"Well, I should," she told me. "I've gone to three different conventions for adopted kids interested in trying to find their biological parents."

"Have you ever thought of changing this into an information brochure?" I asked. "You know, to give adopted kids information and tips on how to start looking for their biological parents?"

"Maybe," Elizabeth said. "That sure would have saved me a lot of time." She finished the story she had begun, but later she went back and wrote that information brochure.

Remember the story "The Little Baldie," which Wayne wrote about his little sister? When Wayne finished, I asked him what he was going to do with it.

"I dunno," he said, shrugging. "Give it to the teacher, I guess."

"Does your mother keep one of those baby

books about your sister?" I asked.

"Yeah, she writes down everything the baby does, first sneeze, first gurgle, first time she rolled over." He rolled his eyes. "Everything."

I suggested that Wayne make a neat copy of his story, maybe even decorate the final piece. Then he could ask his mother if he could tape his story into the baby book. That way when his sister grew up she would be able to read his thoughts about her when she was a baby.

You may be writing something you don't want to share with other readers, and that's fine. But there may be one person out there who would be profoundly affected by your words. Recently I had a writing conference with a fourth grader named Daniel who was writing a book about rainbows. The book had a ton of information about prisms, refraction, and the colors of the spectrum.

"Have you thought about what you're going to do with your writing?" I asked. "The kindergarten kids are just learning about colors. Maybe when you're finished you could visit one of the classes and read it to them."

But Daniel shook his head. "No," he said

politely. "See, my little brother is color-blind. I'm writing this book for him, to teach him about colors."

Daniel's rainbow book won't appear in a bookstore. It will never win a prize. But I don't think his little brother will ever forget it.

THIRTEEN

Writer's Block
and Other Monsters

*I don't know what to write about. I repeat: I do
NOT know what to write about. People keep giving me ideas, but . . . Sigh. If only it was that
easy.*

—Beth Croteau, fourth grade

Yesterday I visited the house we are having built.
The house is about halfway done: The roof is up

and shingled, and two-by-four studs separate the rooms, but that's about it.

The builders had finished their work for the day. I walked alone through the unfinished rooms, breathing the delicious smell of freshly cut wood. Late afternoon sunlight streamed through the cutouts where the windows would be. The blueprints were taped to the wall. I saw many hopeful signs of progress. But the place was trashed! I couldn't believe how many Styrofoam coffee cups, soda cans, bent nails, discarded boxes of screws, cigarette wrappers, scraps of wood, rolls of tape, etc. were scattered on the ground both inside the house and outside. A worker had even left his filthy T-shirt hanging from a board. I knew that in two months the house would be finished, and this mess would be cleaned up. But at that moment, our house-in-progress looked more like a junkyard than Home Sweet Home.

I stood there amidst all the rubbish, trying to be angry about all this, but I couldn't, because I've learned that the same thing is true about my writing process: It's messy. I wish it were nice and neat and orderly. I wish I could say exactly what I want (spelled perfectly and punctuated correctly, of course) the first time I write it. I wish I could instantly come up with the right lead, and have all my information in the right order, but I can't. So I have had to do battle with . . .

Monster # 1: My writing is a hopeless mess! This is one of the first Monsters you run into when you write. You start with a nice clean piece of paper, but after a ton of writing, rewriting, crossing out, etc., your writing looks awful. Sometimes you can barely read what you've written. Get used to that. Messiness is one of the hazards of the trade. Whenever people create something good—whether making a batch of chocolate fudge, writing a story, or building a new house—they usually make a huge mess in the process.

Monster # 2: The needling little voice in your head. When my first son was born I was incredibly happy. I spent hour after hour holding him and staring into that amazing little face. I was keeping a writer's notebook, and most of my entries had something to do with this miniature new person.

One day while looking at my young son, it struck me that a baby's head is sort of like our earth.

The top of the head is like the Arctic tundra—not much growing up there, just a few stray pieces of earth. All the interesting features—mouth, nose, eyes—were scrunched down near the "equator" (the middle of the head).

I liked this comparison. And, being a writer, I wanted to write about it. But as soon as I picked up my pen, this annoying little voice rasped in my ear: *Why waste your time? Do you really think you're the first person to think of that? Believe me, somebody thought of that before! You better find something else to write about.*

Here's how I answered that voice.

"Maybe so," I said. "But maybe not. And anyway, it's the first time that *I* ever thought of it. So I'm going to write it down."

And I did. As a writer, you need to value the way *you* experience the world. Your thoughts, insight, amazement, disgust, etc., will form the foundation of what you write. Tell that annoying little voice to be quiet. Ask it to go out, get a cold soda, and come back later. Much later.

Monster # 3: The low grade blues. In school, when the teacher hands back your writing, you usually see a *B* or *B-* written on top of the first page. But the kid sitting next to you almost always gets an *A*. Why? What's the deal? It is almost as if your writing lacks a magic quality we'll call the *X Factor*. If only you could get some, you could start getting *A*'s, too.

Competing with other kids for higher grades can be frustrating, because some people are naturally better writers than others. When your writing is graded and returned to you, read and carefully consider your teacher's comments. Your teacher is your "writing coach," and a coach can give you invaluable ideas for helping you play the game better. But try not to get too crazy about the actual grade on the piece of writing. Unlike math, writing is not an exact science. Grades in writing often have as much to do with what the teacher likes as what the student writes. It's more important that *you* get a feel for when your writing is good, or where you did less than your best work.

Monster # 4: The not-so-great American novel. The problem here is being too ambitious in your writing. When you were little—say around first grade—your reading and your writing were roughly on the same level. You could read/write a simple story. By fourth grade most kids are reading long novels. Many junior or senior high-school kids read sci-fi, fantasy, horror, or thrillers that are six or eight hundred pages long. When you're reading novels, you may want to write a novel of your own. Be cautious. It can be fun to try, but for most students, writing a novel is biting off more than they can chew—way more. You get confused, you get lost, you get overwhelmed by the project.

Imagine being a twelve-year-old who loves to play baseball, and who goes to the major leagues and gets struck out by Pedro Martinez. Would you be disappointed? Sure. But it's no reason to quit playing baseball! If you really do want to try writing a chapter book or novel, proceed in a spirit of fun and adventure. Think small. Try to look at each part of the book as a separate chunk. Don't beat yourself up if you end up abandoning the project.

Monster # 5: Writer's block. Arghh! NOTHING TO WRITE ABOUT! Have you seen this cruel creature? Has it inflicted torture on your soul while you sat during writing time with nothing on the paper (and even less in your head)? Well, you're not alone. By some freak of nature, I almost never battle this beast, but most writers do. Let's take a look at how this group of students battle writer's block when it rears its ugly head.

"My brain is sometimes exploding with ideas," says Corey Thom, a fourth grader. "Other times it's like a desert full of sand. For those times I consult . . . the Great and Powerful Book of My Notebook! This is where I keep my list of thirteen ways to get an idea."

"When I'm stuck, I get ideas from watching my guinea pig, Snowball," says Evelyn Tang, a sixth grader. "I feed her veggies from the kitchen, usually the Chinese vegetable kind, her favorite. I watch her munching away, and if I listen carefully, her rapid chewing sounds like a miniature pencil sharpener that's constantly grinding away at a pencil. While I am just sitting quietly, a marvelous idea pops into my head. When she is just lazily squatting in her cage, I realize how she doesn't have to do any work. No homework, no school, and all she does is eat, play with her ball, get petted, and sleep. The easy life of a guinea pig from its perspective will be the idea for the poem that I want to write."

"I find that doodling is the best cure for writer's block," says eighth grader Zack Wells. "Nine times out of ten, if I draw or doodle for fifteen minutes I get an idea for something to write about."

"When I have writer's block I go away from the writing altogether," says Zoë Wollenberg, a sixth grader. "A brain is a pretty amazing thing. Even when I'm really not thinking about my writing, my brain works on it way back in the deepest, darkest corner that I never knew I had. When I'm doing something totally unrelated, playing the piano, listening to music, or reading my orca book, an idea will come to me when I'm least expecting it."

I think of writer's block as nothing to write about, but this problem can also show up when you're smack in the middle of a story.

"Whenever I'm in the middle of a really cool story and I can't find the words or pictures I need to keep going, I run outside and gently sway on the swings," says sixth grader Emily Mintz. "I drag my toes through the cold mud and dive into the story I'm writing. As I rock back and forth, I start to feel the rhythm of the ideas . . ."

When dealing with writer's block, the trick may be to stay calm, resist that feeling of intense frustration, and try to look at it as a good thing.

"Writer's block is a quiet place where you can sit and soak in the silence," says author Drew Lamm. "Sometimes you need to get there to refresh or refuel or just to listen to a cardinal's song. It's also a good place to sit when reading a brilliant book (though I prefer a soft chair). Then when you are refreshed, you get up, wave good-bye to the block, and pick up your pen again."

Last Thoughts

My brother Jim is a sculptor. He works with metal, including silicon bronze, but he has also carved some marvelous sculptures from wood.

He begins with an idea in his head and a big chunk of wood. Using a number of different knives, Jim starts carving into the wood. The knives are razor sharp, so he works carefully. Soon the floor of his garage or a studio is covered with slivers of wood cut from the original block. He works like that for hours or even days. At times he steps back from the sculpture, looking at the figure or shape emerging from the wood. He starts again, cutting more here and there, until finally he's got exactly the shape he wants.

Now it's time to polish. Jim smooths the wood with sandpaper, first coarse, then finer and finer grades, until it feels smooth to the touch. You'd think he would be finished by then, but he's not. He pours oil onto the wood ("Each kind of wood drinks up a different amount of oil," he told me once), and then rubs the wood with a soft piece of cloth. When he's finished, the wood glows and you can see the lovely grain of the wood.

It's interesting to compare Jim's procedure for sculpting with the process that writers use. He starts with an idea (brainstorm), cuts the wood (rough draft), stands back to see what he's done (rereading), makes some changes (revision) until he's satisfied that he has the shape right. Only then does he start to polish (proofread and edit). Jim can sell the finished sculpture (publish), display it at an art gallery, or give it away. Sometimes he enters it in an art show, where it gets judged (graded).

In this book I've tried to help you find a way of writing that is tailored to you, your personality, quirks, strengths, and, yes, your weaknesses. Find a process that feels comfortable, but don't carve it in granite, either. Your writing process will probably change as you get older, have new experiences, read different kinds of books. Your writing process should be flexible enough to grow with you.

With enough time and practice this process will become invisible. You'll hardly think about how you're writing. Instead, your attention will be laser-focused on the subject you're writing about.

You can talk and talk about the process writers use to write, but you can't forget that real feeling is still the crucial ingredient. You need to feel the words, feel the sentences, feel the ideas and characters. They need to matter to you. Author Mem Fox reminds us that a writer needs to "ache with caring" over a piece of writing. Wise words! The goal is to be totally engaged in the work and play of writing, so you can put your whole heart into making something real, lasting, beautiful. That's a worthwhile thing to do.

Selected Reading

Fletcher, Ralph. *A Writer's Notebook: Unlocking the Writer within You.* Avon Books, 1996.

Fletcher, Ralph. *Have You Been to the Beach Lately?* Orchard Books, 2001.

Fletcher, Ralph. *Live Writing: Breathing Life into Your Words.* Avon Books, 1999.

Fletcher, Ralph. *Ordinary Things: Poems from a Walk in Early Spring.* Atheneum, 1997.

Fletcher, Ralph. *Tommy Trouble and the Crystal Mumbo Jumbo.* Henry Holt, 2000.

Fletcher, Ralph. *Where Can You Find a New Nose?*

Henderson, Kathy. *Market Guide for Young Writers.* Betterway Publications, 1993.

Korman, Gordon. *Liar, Liar, Pants on Fire.* Scholastic, 1997.

Korman, Gordon. *Nose Pickers from Outer Space.* Disney, 1999.

Korman, Gordon. *The Chicken Doesn't Skate.* Scholastic, 1998.

Korman, Gordon. *This Can't Be Happening at MacDonald Hall.* Scholastic, 1996.

Lamm, Drew. *Prog Frince: A Mixed-Up Tale.* Orchard Books, 1999.

Lamm, Drew. *Sea Lion Roars.* Soundprints, 1997.

Lamm, Drew. "Stay True." In *Stay True: Short Stories for Strong Girls.* Edited by Marilyn Singer. Scholastic, 1999.

Mikaelsen, Ben. *Countdown.* Hyperion, 1996.

Mikaelsen, Ben. *Petey.* Hyperion, 1998.

Mikaelsen, Ben. *Rescue Josh McGuire.* Hyperion, 1991.

Nolan, Jerdine. *Harvey Potter's Balloon Farm.* Lothrop, Lee & Shepard, 1994.